World of Reading

2

Disney
ZOMBIES 2
CALL TO THE WILD

Adapted by
Steve Behling

Based on the Disney Channel Original Movie by
David Light and Joseph Raso

Welcome to Seabrook!
Meet Zed and his sister, Zoey.
They are zombies.
People used to think
zombies were monsters.

But not anymore!
Zed and Zoey can go
wherever they want.
They can even buy their
favorite zombie ice cream.

Addison and her best friend
are going to cheer camp.
Addison's cousin leads
the Mighty Shrimp cheer squad.

He wants everyone
to be like him.
Addison is different.
She wants everyone to just
be themselves.

Zombies run the old
Seabrook power plant.
The town plans to tear it down.
Everyone is glad to see it go.

Well, not everyone.
Zed's best friend, Eliza,
says the power plant is an
important part of zombie history.

Zed has something special to do.
He is asking Addison to Prawn.
Prawn is a dance party, like prom.
This year, zombies can go.

Zed hangs a sign along the road. Addison will see it when the bus comes home from cheer camp.

But the bus doesn't see Zed!
He gets knocked off his ladder
and lands on top of the bus.
Luckily, Zed isn't hurt.

But the bus smashes through
a fence and off the road.
Addison and her friends
find themselves in a dark forest.

Addison wants to make sure
that Zed is okay.
She looks for him in the forest.
Little does she know
that she is being watched!

Suddenly, there's a loud howl.
AWOOOOOOOOOO!
Werewolves are in the forest!
All of Seabrook is afraid
of werewolves.

Zed asks Addison to Prawn.
She wants to say yes, but she
tells him that monsters can't go.
Seabrook's anti-monster laws
are back on!

That means no werewolves,
and no zombies, either!
Zed will find a way to take
Addison to the dance.

The werewolves think
Addison might be able to help
them find their lost moonstone.

The wolf pack shows up
at Seabrook High.
What will the werewolves do?

Everyone is ready for a big fight with the werewolves.

But the werewolves don't want
to fight.
They just want to join the school.

Addison talks to the werewolves.
They tell her about the moonstone.
The werewolves need it to survive.
Addison wants to help them.

The werewolves invite
Addison to their wolf den.
She isn't afraid to go
into the forest with them.

The werewolves tell Addison
about a special person
who might save them.
Addison looks just like her!

The werewolves give Addison
a makeover.
Now she feels like one of them.

Zed and his friends are worried.

Where is Addison?

Did the werewolves take her?

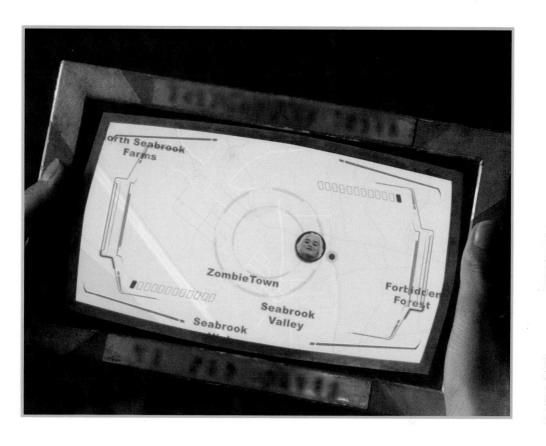

Eliza tracks Addison's cell phone.
The friends think the werewolves
might hurt her.
But they're wrong.
The werewolves want Addison
to join them.

Zed and his friends find Addison.
She thinks the moonstone is
beneath the power plant.
If the town destroys the building,
the moonstone might be lost!

The werewolves go to
the power plant to stop it
from being destroyed.
The Z-Patrol tries to arrest them.

Suddenly, Addison, Zed,
and their friends arrive.
They convince the town
not to destroy the power plant.

But something goes wrong.
The power plant is destroyed.
The werewolves think
their moonstone is gone forever!

At last, Prawn arrives.
The humans, zombies, and
werewolves all go to the dance.

Suddenly, the ground erupts.
Everyone joins the werewolves
to search for the moonstone.
Together, they find the
powerful stone.

With the moonstone found,
the werewolves will survive.
And Prawn can continue.
All the kids dance, because
Addison brought them together.